Robin's Ring

Jeanette Taylor Ford

Cover and

Interior Illustrations by

Kathryn Green

Other cover magic by

Mr Dave Slaney

LONGSHIP
Publishing

For Megan, Reuben, Charlie, India and Katieleigh

Thank you for your interest and suggestions. I hope you like this finished production.

Author's Note

This story was originally written to encourage children living in my area of Nottingham to get interested in their own surroundings. Therefore, all the places mentioned in this book are real and the legends that are around them are as mentioned in this book.

Chapter 1

The Scattering

Long, Long Ago

The peaceful stillness of the night was abruptly shattered with shouts and screams. The figure slumbering in the shadowy low bed, laden with furs, sat up and then swung his legs quickly off his cosy nest. Orvin hurried from the pile of furs and, although he had his clothes on, pulled a heavy cloak from a chair, wrapped it around himself and dragged open the door of his room.

He ran down the corridor, all the time listening to the sounds of running feet and shouts. Reaching another door, he burst in and slammed it shut behind him. There was a man in the room, a figure whose face glowed and golden hair shone. He wore white robes and round his waist was a golden girdle. He held some objects in his hands and was already busy with them. Without preamble and barely looking up he said,

"There thou art, Orvin - barricade the door! We have but a short time."

Orvin turned towards the door and waved his hands towards it, chanting words beneath his breath.

"It won't hold for long, master, thou dost know my magic is not as strong as thine."

"No matter, as long as it buys me enough time to hide the Items of Power before our enemy, Bowen, can stop me."

Even as he spoke, the door began to shudder under powerful blows. In the room there came the sound of soft chanting and there was a sudden rush of light, a tiny thing like a red shooting star lit the room for a moment as it left the Golden Man's hand and was gone almost as soon as it had appeared. A moment later, a larger, yellow light did the same; it seemed to hang in the air for a moment and then was gone in a whoosh.

The door held fast in spite of the assault upon it. In haste the two men moved again upon hearing the shouts of those behind the door and a louder one: 'stand back, thou fools!"

Orvin's magic sealing of the door disintegrated in a puff of smoke and, as the intruders burst into the room, they were just in time to see a narrow golden light about three feet long lie in the air before them and then shoot away into the darkness above them. They halted in awe for a few moments at the unexpected spectacle before them.

A dark figure, dressed all in black, pushed into the room. Another man followed him, carrying a fiery torch.

Orvin positioned himself in front of his master, hands splayed. He sent a bolt of electricity at the men's feet. They jumped.

"Stop him, fools!"

The other men were galvanised into action and others joined them as they leaped towards Orvin and his master and grabbed them, twisting their arms behind their backs. No amount of struggling helped; they were outnumbered and held fast. The dark man went up to the golden figure.

"So – thou thought thou could outwit me! As thou can see, I am more powerful than thee – I have broken thy puny protections. Now, give me them!"

The golden man looked the man in the eyes.

"I do not have them."

He reeled under the sudden blow to his face.

"Liar!"

Orvin struggled again at the sight of his master being treated thus. It did no good, only made his captor's hold on him tighter still.

"Master," one of the men holding the Golden Man said timidly, "we saw something disappear as we came in."

"Ah, using thy pathetic magic to hide them art thou? Give them to me."

"I cannot; I told thee, I do not have them. They are now lost in time; I cannot get them but neither can thee. I would die rather than let thee have them."

"Do not tempt me thus or thou wilt regret it!" Bowen the Black punched the golden man in his stomach, and, as he doubled over with the pain, there was the sudden glint of something at his wrist. Before he could do anything, Bowen pounced upon it.

"What do we have here then? Thou hast been lying again, methinks."

He wrenched it off the other man's wrist, with the help of the guards who held his arms.

"Well, this is something — perchance it will help me obtain the other Items. Leave them now; we have at least one thing we came for."

So saying, he turned and strode out of the room. The men holding the two captives pushed them to the floor and kicked them. Then they followed their master.

As they did so, Orvin scrambled to his feet to go after them but Edric his master weakly called him back.

"Let them go; there is nothing thou can do now, come and help me."

So the servant turned back to tend to his master and gave a gasp as he looked at him. The once-golden man was now as dark and ordinary as himself. The light had gone out.

Chapter 2

Recovery Plans

"Master – what's happened to thee?" His master was indeed a sight; his right cheek swollen and bruised, his eye closed. He was also doubled in pain from the punch and the kicking he had received.

"Help me up, wilt thou?"

The servant helped his master to sit up and then gradually to stand up. Together they hobbled over to the bed, where he gently laid the injured man down again.

"Do not agitate thyself, Orvin, I will soon be well again. Send for Moriah, she will see me right. And then we must make our plans."

"Plans, my lord?"

"Yes, my faithful friend — we must recover the amulet without delay. The longer it is in the hands of Bowen the Black, the greater the danger there might be of losing all the Items of Power and if that happens it will be the end of me and of our kin."

The servant looked at his master for a moment frowning, then he bowed.

"I will fetch Moriah at once; as thou sayest, we must hurry."

He hastened from the room and the other man allowed himself to relax on the bed. He must gather his strength for what they had to do next...

It was but a few minutes before Orvin came hurrying back, in his wake was a woman dressed in a long silver dress with a dark blue cloak. She hurried to the bedside to examine the man.

"Oh my Lord - thou art indeed a sight! But do not worry; Moriah will soon make thee well."

She held her hand lightly over his face, muttering words under her breath. She closed her eyes, breathing deeply and then she removed her hand slowly. There was no longer any swelling or bruising and his face looked quite normal again. Then she slowly waved her hands over his body, still murmuring the strange incantations.

Under Orvin's gaze, his lord gradually straightened out, all sign of pain disappearing. He was now relaxed completely, his eyes shut and breathing evenly.

"He will sleep for a very short time and when he wakes he will be completely cured of his injuries," Moriah arose to her feet as she spoke, "now let me look at thee, Orvin."

In spite of his protests that he was fine, Moriah insisted and eventually he sat down on a short bench obediently. She ran her hands over him in the air as she had done before.

"Hmm, just as I thought, thy left leg is injured and thou hast some bruising to thy stomach. Hold still," she ordered. She shut her eyes and proceeded to murmur again, holding one hand on his shin where he had been kicked. He winced a little as he felt first a fiery pain and then nothing. Her hands moved up to above his stomach area and again he felt the heat but it wasn't so painful this time. When she stopped, he looked at her gratefully.

"Thou wilt be fine now my son." She put her arms around his shoulders and he laid his head against her for a moment.

"What would we do without thee, my mother?"

She laughed, "I do not know."

Then she nodded towards the bed.

"Make sure you look after him my son; he is healed but his power has been greatly reduced."

He nodded. Moriah gave his shoulder a last gentle pat and left the room. Orvin watched her go and then turned his attention to the figure on the bed. As he walked over to the bed, the man stirred; it was obvious he was waking up already. He sat up and swung around in order to put his feet on the ground.

"Oh, that is much better. Thy mother is wonderful, Orvin, what would we do without her?"

Orvin chuckled. "That's just what I said to her a few moments ago. Art thou really well now, my lord?"

"Oh yes, I am feeling strong again now."

"What happened? Why aren't you shining and golden?"

"Because of the absence of the Items of Power, Orvin. I still have much power but it has been greatly reduced because I no longer have them. But they belong to me and could well be dangerous in the wrong hands. The other Items are safe; the ring will find a worthy wearer to work for us. But the Amulet has been taken; we cannot allow it to remain in the hands of our enemy Bowen the Black and his followers. Who knows what damage they will do with it, we must recover it without delay."

"Why did thee not use thy magic against them? Thou art much stronger than he will ever be."

"I did not want him to know that; sometimes it is best to let thine enemies think thou art weaker than they. In can be good strategy."

Orvin nodded thoughtfully, that made sense to him.

"How are we going to recover the Amulet?"

"We will consult the Silver Crystal immediately to see where they have taken it. Come."

Edric strode from the room with Orvin following but a step behind him.

Hurrying down a long golden lined corridor the torches burning in sconces on the walls casting bright patches and eerie darker ones as they moved along, they came to a stairway that they hastened down. Muttering words and sweeping his hand around in a circle, a door suddenly appeared before them and swung open. Without losing pace, they entered the room, which was dark but had a glint of silver that caught the eye in the centre of the room. It was in fact a large piece of rock which was embedded in the floor. In the top of it was a sparkling crystal, as big as a hand mirror with a silvery sheen. It was a very unusual crystal as they are usually glassy and clear or various colours such a black, blue or amethyst. This was one of a kind.

The two men stood either side of the rock and Orvin watched as his master peered intently into the crystal.

"Oh Silver Crystal, so clear and bright

Show where the amulet was taken this night"

Moments later:

"Right, I have it. He thinks his power is greater than mine especially now. But even without the Items of Power I'm still more powerful than he. We will give him a shock, Orvin my friend! Come, let us leave."

"Shouldn't we take others with us to help, my lord?"

"No. We will accomplish more if we go alone. Fear not, we have right on our side."

Without another word, the two men left the room swiftly.

Chapter 3

Robin

Present Day

"Oh Robin – are you watching that *again?*"

Robin looked up as his mother came into the room. He had been so lost, deep in the film, that he hadn't even heard her come in. Carole worked in a shoe shop and so she always arrived home after him, but he was a sensible boy and always let himself into the house after school, made a sandwich and a drink and settled to do his homework. After that, he allowed himself to do the things he loved best – either reading a book or watching a film on DVD.

His mum stood for a few moments, watching the film as Sam watched with horror as the gnomes, or whatever they were, took Frodo away with them, all cocooned in the webbing from the giant spider that Sam had just had a fight with.

"I just don't know how you can keep watching it, Robin; it's really horrible in some places."

"I know," Robin grinned, "but I know what happens so it's okay. I love it; it's such a great story. I loved reading it but watching it is wonderful; the effects are amazing."

Carole turned to go out of the room. "Well, it's all right for some people I suppose, being glued to the television screen! I have to get dinner on; your dad will be home in an hour."

Robin turned his attention back to the screen as his mother left the room, shutting the door behind her.

As she gathered the ingredients for the meal, Carole shook her head as she thought about Robin's love for adventure films and books.

She wished he could be outside playing football or something with other boys, but he was not able to do that as he had severe health problems which meant he was not strong and could not play like other boys. He was quite clever though; his long times of illness meant he read a lot and he knew a great deal about many things. However, she knew he would much rather be able to play football...

Robin's dad arrived home from his work in an insurance office about six. He always looked for Robin when he got home but of course he knew what his son would be doing!

"Honestly son," he laughed, "You've watched that film so often, you will turn into a hobbit one day!"

"Oh, I wish dad! I wish I could find a ring and have amazing adventures like that. Just imagine what it would be like to have a magic ring."

"Ah yes, but that ring is not good is it? Although it makes the wearer invisible, it also turns their hearts black – and look what it did to poor Gollum – you wouldn't like to go like that would you?"

"Oh no, that's true dad, I would hate to be like him. If I had a magic ring, I would like it to do good things."

His dad patted him on the shoulder.

"Well, I'm sure if you had one, it would. Unfortunately, magic doesn't really exist. Unless we're talking about your mum's cooking that is! Come on son, let's go and see what she's got for us."

When Robin lay in bed that night, waiting for sleep to come, he thought about the film and about The Ring. He allowed his imagination to carry him away and he was off adventuring with Frodo, Sam and the others, into a world where there was magic, black and white, great good and terrible evil...

Chapter 4

The Discovery

He never expected to find one in the garden – after all, who finds magic rings in their own garden? Robin and his dad had dug and worked in the garden many times and never found anything, except an old spoon and a huge frog. They looked for the frog every year; he lived under an old tyre at the very bottom of the garden which collected rainwater in the middle like a tiny pond; his very own private pool.

It was spring and Robin and his dad were working, preparing the beds for the vegetables that dad would be planting. Robin couldn't dig, but he used a trowel and knelt down beside the bed, picking out the weeds that had been loosened by dad's forking. He suddenly saw something silver showing in the earth. He carefully dug it out with his trowel and looked at what he'd found – it was a ring.

Robin looked at the dirty object in his hand; he couldn't believe it – he had found a ring of his very own! Could it possibly be magic?

"Look what I've found dad," Robin held his hand out towards his dad, the ring sitting in his palm.

"Well, look at that! How come that was in the garden I wonder?" Roy picked the ring out of his son's hand and examined it closely. "I think it needs a good clean."

"Can I have it dad? Please?"

"Of course you can have it son; I don't suppose it's worth anything. If it was in the leaf mould that we collected off Church Close it probably came from the fair that comes to St. Giles' Park every year."

"I 'spect so dad, but I still want it - can I go and clean it now?"

"Oh yes lad, go on." Roy looked after his son as he limped excitedly down the garden to the house, shook his head in amusement and carried on with his digging.

Robin watched as the earth washed away from the ring and down the sink. He rubbed it with his fingers until he was sure he had all the dirt off it. Just as he was drying his hands, his mum came into the kitchen.

"Hello love, what have you got there?" Carole peered at the ring on the draining board.

"It's a ring; I just found it in the garden. Dad said I could have it."

"Did he now?" Mum picked up the ring and looked closely at it, turning it round and round.

"I have some special stuff that will really clean this and make it shiny. Would you like me to do it for you?"

"Oh yes please mum."

Robin watched his mum as she got the cleaning fluid out, tipped a little onto a piece of cloth and rubbed the ring with it. She applied the fluid all over the ring, and then she got another cloth and rubbed it some more.

As his mum worked on the ring, Robin could hear a sort of high humming sound – was it coming from the ring? Robin looked at his mum as she concentrated on her task – could she hear it too? She didn't look as though she did. He was used to hearing strange sounds in his ears because of the ear trouble he had; the doctors called it 'tinnitus,' He decided that it must be that; it's just that the sound was different to what he'd heard before...

Mum held it up so that Robin could see the newly polished ring. It shone all sparkly silver; Robin thought it was very pretty. She handed it to him and he held it in the palm of his hand admiring it; it felt warm, no doubt the result of all the rubbing.

"Thanks mum."

Carole laughed as he rushed off to his room. No doubt Robin would be thinking up lots more imaginary adventures now that he had his very own ring.

Chapter 5

Knowledge of the Ring

The ring did, indeed, help Robin to imagine more adventures. He imagined that it was gold and very precious and he was the keeper of it, like Frodo, and had to protect it from others who tried to get it.

A couple of days after the ring had been found, Robin returned home from school, dragging his feet and struggling to breathe. They had just ended the day with P.E. and it had brought on his asthma. He had his inhaler with him and it helped some, but Mr Brown had pushed them harder and harder. He was a supply teacher and didn't know much about Robin. When the boys tried to point it out to him, he simply told Robin to rest for a few minutes, then ordered him to resume the running they had just been doing. As it was, he struggled to run with his bad leg, but Mr Brown just kept egging him on.

He let himself into the house, knowing his mum wouldn't be there. He was so tired; he went straight upstairs, dragging himself slowly and painfully up each one, stopping to gasp in breaths every time. It took him a long time to get up all the stairs.

Thankfully, he lay down on his bed, propped up by his pillows. There were extra pillows always kept in his room for just such a time as this as Robin found it even more difficult to breathe lying down. As he laid there, waiting and hoping his breathing would ease, he heard that strange, high-pitched but musical sound he thought he heard the other day when mum was cleaning his ring. He turned his head to look at it on his bedside table.

That's funny – he could have sworn the ring looked a red-gold colour, sort of glowing...

He reached out and picked it up, slipping it onto the middle finger of his right hand. He held it up to look at it more closely.

As he did so, he realised his breathing became easier; in fact, his chest felt clearer than he had ever known it to be. He sat up abruptly, and swung his legs off the bed. Then he realised that his bad leg seemed to be as straight and strong as his other one – in fact, he could feel strength coursing through him and he felt like a prize-fighter. He had never felt so fit and strong in his life.

Robin sat and thought for a moment. Then, he slipped the ring off his finger and put it back on the bedside table. His breathing became laboured and his leg was again twisted and puny. He quickly put the ring back on again and loved the feeling of the strength pouring back into his body.

Wow – his ring really *was* magic! There – he had always known it somehow. And if he wore it for PE lessons he would *really* show Mr Brown. Robin was so excited; he would be able to play football and do all sorts of things.

Then, he suddenly realised that he couldn't do that; he would never be allowed to wear the ring at school – if a teacher saw it they would confiscate it. There was no way he could or would run the risk of losing the ring. Nor could he play football with the lads with it on; he would be too strong for them, he just knew he would be. And if he played footie with his mates, they would wonder why he couldn't manage PE... no, he knew he could not use it in public. But he was sure there would be times when he could use it – and he was certainly grateful to it now.

He was bursting to tell his parents, but then suddenly he just knew it wasn't right to tell them either; somehow he knew the ring didn't want him to.

Chapter 6
Oliver

Robin rushed down the stairs as fast as his bad leg would let him when he heard the doorbell.

He opened the door.

"Hey, Ol – you've come at last – cool."

Robin's cousin Oliver, who was a bit older than Robin, had come to stay for the Easter holidays. Oliver's and Robin's mums were sisters. The boys had always been good pals and Oliver never let Robin's disabilities deter them from doing things together.

"Hey Rob, what have you got planned for us to do today then, mate?" Oliver dumped his bag on the floor and followed his cousin into the kitchen.

"I thought we could go to Bramcote Hills Park, have some adventuring there, explore the woods and take a picnic."

"Sounds good – that's one of my favourite places."

"Mine too. Shall we ask mum to pack us a picnic then?"

"Of course."

The boys waited patiently for mum to make them some food, even though they were eager to be off. She was going to pop them over to the park in the car and then collect them later. She knew they would be all right; after all, they were both ten and were quite sensible. She never worried about Robin when he was with Oliver.

It was about eleven o'clock when they finally set off but it didn't take long to get there.

"Do you have everything – food, jackets, mobile phones and your inhaler, Robin?

"And my ring," He thought, fingering it in his pocket but said out loud: "Yes mum, we have everything we need. See you later."

"Five, okay? Call me if you want to come home before then."

"Will do. Bye!"

Mum waved as she drove off but the boys were already heading towards the walled garden. She smiled. She knew they would shortly be off to the Land of Mordor, or other similarly gruesome place...

The boys changed their minds and veered off towards the play area and spent a great couple of hours climbing, swinging and doing all the things kids do on play apparatus. Eventually, they decided to stop and eat so they went off to sit at a picnic table that was available. They spread the food out on the table.

"Cor, Rob, Aunty Carole has certainly gone to town with the grub, mate! There's no way we can eat all this now."

"Don't matter, Ol," Robin picked up a ham sandwich. "We'll save some for later; have some in the woods. We should always have supplies for an emergency you know."

"That's right; we should be prepared properly for travelling through unknown territory."

There was silence while the boys ate with intent and then they packed up what was left in their back-packs, threw the rubbish in a nearby bin and set off excitedly by mutual consent towards the woods, or rather, the Forbidden Wood... What were they going to encounter – a huge spider, a giant, a unicorn – or something quite unexpected...?

A couple of hours later, the boys were embedded in an adventure they never could have imagined would really happen to them...

Chapter 7

The Adventures Begin

An hour or so later, the boys were making their way higher and higher through the woods.

"Hang on a minute, Ol, I need to stop and have a puff," Robin stopped, panting. He felt in his pocket for his inhaler and, giving it a shake, he put it to his mouth. His shoulders were hunched and his chest was squeaking. Oliver felt bad, he should never have let Rob come up this far! He watched as Robin took his second puff.

"It's okay Ol, I'll be fine in a minute." Robin slipped the inhaler back into his pocket and, as he did so, he felt the ring — of course! He slid his finger into it in his pocket. Immediately, he felt the power as strength flowed into him. He must be careful; he mustn't let Oli see it happening all at once.

With a supreme effort, he gradually let his breathing ease as if it was happening as the result of the Ventalin. His leg felt so much better too, no longer aching terribly as it had a few moments ago. He straightened up.

"I'm fine now- let's go!" And he set off again at a pace. Before long, he could hear Oliver panting behind him.

"Hey, hey Rob - you turned into Superman or somethin'? Hang on, I can't keep up, take it steady or you'll be ill — or I will."

Robin slowed his step, and then he stopped. Oliver bumped into his back.

"Oof! You could have warned me you were going to stop!"

"Sorry, Ol, but I am puzzled — don't you think the wood is thicker than it used to be? I could have sworn we were on the path that went round the edge — we should be able to see over the quarry now, but I can't see anything except trees."

Oliver looked round.

"Yes, I think you're right. That's funny. We can't be where we thought we were. Better keep walking; we will get somewhere eventually; surely we can't be far from the road now."

The boys walked on in silence, hoping they were going the right way. The feeling of being lost was making them feel as though maybe they were not so sure about adventures now. The path was dipping; they thought the road must surely be near, but there seemed to be no let-up in the trees, no gaps showing through. The path went quite low down and then it started to go up again. Robin was fine because he was wearing his ring, but Oliver was getting tired and fed up — and not a little worried about where they might be. They must have got on the wrong path somehow — were they going round in circles perhaps? It didn't feel like it. He brought his mobile phone out of his pocket and looked at it. There was no signal. He hoped they wouldn't need to call Rob's mum...

Suddenly, without warning it seemed, the trees stopped and they were in a small clearing. Strangely, it was much darker than it had been, as if it was evening – but it couldn't be, it was still the afternoon surely?

They looked about them curiously. The landscape was completely unfamiliar; they had no idea at all where they were. They crossed the clearing because they could see there was another one beyond a few more trees. As they came to the edge of the line of trees, they could see something on top of a bare hill that looked vaguely familiar.

"Crikey Ol, I think that's the Hemlock Stone!"

"Wow, mate, I think you're right! But it doesn't look right; it isn't on top of a hill like this and there should be trees much closer than they are."

Robin peered at the strange rocky column, straining to see it in the evening gloom.

"It's bigger at the base and it's not so black at the top – it looks just like normal stone!"

"So it does. That's strange. Did you know they had changed it?"

"Of course they haven't changed it! How could they? Even if they somehow cleaned the top, they couldn't make the bottom bigger could they – it's sandstone."

The boys looked at each other. As they did so, they could see people coming over the hill towards the stone, some of them carrying what looked like torches of fire, held aloft.

Robin's ring hummed loudly; he looked down at it. It was no longer red-gold, it was bright red – red was for danger wasn't it? What could it mean?

Chapter 8

Adventurous Night.

Edric and Orvin crept as silently as they could through the night. It had taken them some time to reach their destination, sheltering hidden in the woods during the daytime out of harm's way. Now, Orvin felt the prickle down his neck as he realised they were where they needed to be. Now they had to exercise even more caution. Orvin followed his master's lead as they moved silently towards the cave cut into the rock amongst the trees. Further back, they could see the dark shapes of round huts. This was where Bowen the Black resided, in this cave, his servants in the huts below.

"He will have the amulet in the cave. We must find a way to get in there and look."

"How will we do that, Master? It will be guarded all the time. I would think it's unlikely he will leave the amulet unattended. What if he is wearing it?"

"Don't worry about that, my friend. He will have discovered by now that he cannot wear it. All the Items of Power choose who they will be held by or worn by. It will not let him put it on. No, that at least we do not have to worry about."

"We have enough to concern us about getting in there. Can't you use magic, Master?"

"Not as yet, it's too dangerous. No, we will lie low and see what happens. Come."

Edric withdrew to a rock formation that provided them shelter from every side with comfort to sit in between.

"We can relax for a while and have some food. I am sure something will happen to help us soon." He reached into a small bag he was carrying and withdrew two large pieces of bread and some chunks of cheese. Orvin had long since got used to this bag of Edric's that could produce things much larger than it should hold. He knew it was magic of course and Edric could take anything he wanted from it. He tucked into the food without question, keeping a watchful eye on the scene below them.

Although it was dark, they could just make out figures that moved between the huts and they could also see the flicker of flames within some of them, indicating the residents were cooking. As they sat there, an owl hooted and the wind rustled the trees gently. The two men, tired from their activities, began to feel drowsy.

Orvin jumped violently when Edric grabbed his arm.

"Look!"

Orvin peered between the rocks in order to see what Edric meant. There was a flurry of activity amongst the huts; people were gathering, some carrying flaming torches. They gathered outside the cave. Before long, a figure in a long dark cloak with a hood emerged from the cave and several others came behind him, also carrying torches. One of them carried a chicken, yet another had a bowl.

The waiting crowd, as one, slipped hoods on their heads too and, as the imposing leader moved away from the cave, everyone else fell into line behind him. The two men watched silently from behind the rocks as the procession passed by them, the sounds of chanting rising in the air. Orvin shuddered and Edric placed a hand on his friend's shoulder. They stayed where they were, looking at the backs of the procession as they gradually paced away from the hill the cave was on. Soon, they could see nothing as the lights from the torches gradually faded away into the enveloping darkness.

Edric sprang to life.

"We have no time to lose! They will not be long once they have sacrificed that poor bird. We must find the amulet."

Edric crept towards the cave. As he did so, a man came out.

"Who is there?" He was almost immediately silenced by Orvin who landed on him from above, swiftly giving him a hefty blow, rendering him unconscious. They dragged him out of sight behind some bushes and then made their way back to the cave. This time, there was no one to apprehend them. Obviously, Bowen thought that it was safe to leave the amulet so under-guarded.

A ball of light went before them as they walked deeper into the cave. Edric pulled from his bag a round piece of crystal. He looked deep into it and then said, "this way." Taking a left fork in the tunnels, he walked briskly down it, Orvin following at his heels. Before too long, the tunnel opened out into a cave. And there, under a sparkling dome, was the amulet. Orvin went over to it, meaning to lift the dome, only to emit an anguished howl as it bit into his fingers.

"Curses! It has a magic spell on it."

"Of course it does my friend; that's why he thought it was safe to leave it. But this is old, worn out magic. Easy." He waved his hands over the dome, just above it, muttering words under his breath. In a few moments, the dome appeared to melt away, allowing Edric to pick up the amulet. He tucked it into his bag, waved his hands again over the dome, muttering some more. The dome hardened and appeared to still have the amulet underneath. Orvin looked at it admiringly. No one could match his master for magic.

"Now we must hasten away from here." Edric and Orvin hastened back the way they had come. As they neared the entrance of the cave, they could hear the murmur of voices drawing closer. Edric's ball of light went out swiftly and they shrank back into the shadows. Their hearts were in their mouths as they stood there. Were they going to be discovered?

Edric started a low muttering; Orvin knew he was casting a spell. Moments later, he could no longer see the dark shape of his master beside him. They were invisible.

"Quick! The spell does not last long, we must go as fast as we can."

They ran as fast as their legs would carry them. Some of the people looked puzzled as they felt something move swiftly past them but they could see nothing. The two men ran into the trees and kept going as long as they could, until they had to sink down on a fallen log to rest. As they did so, Orvin saw his master gradually reappear and imagined he did too. They looked at each other and laughed.

"We did it!"

Chapter 9

Captured!

"Keep down!" Robin hissed to Oliver urgently. Oliver didn't need any urging; he was increasingly worried about what was happening. The boys watched from their position crouched in the undergrowth as a large group of people wearing black clothes and hoods emerged, holding their torches high. They were not near enough for the boys to see their faces, shadowed as they were by their hoods. They gathered around the Hemlock Stone, looking small against the towering height of the rock and, before long, they seemed to be performing some sort of ritual, singing and bowing. The ones that seemed in charge had a chicken and a bowl.

The lads heard the chicken's cry of distress suddenly stop and they realised, sickeningly, that the bird had been killed. They were not near enough to see what was happening and they were thankful. They wondered how long they would have to be there; time seemed to pass very slowly as they hardly dared to breathe.

As they sat in the gathering darkness, Oliver's attention wandered away from the scene before them. He noticed the ring, still glowing red on Robin's hand.

"What's that?" he whispered.

Robin realised he had been so taken up with the happenings in the clearing that he'd forgotten to hide his ring. He also realised that there was little point in trying to hide it now. He put his finger up to his mouth:

"Sh – I'll tell you later."

His mind was working rapidly; he already knew the ring could give him strength. He also realised that it wasn't until he put it on that the woods started to become unfamiliar. Could it be the ring doing this? Could it have taken them back in time? He had read that Druids were supposed to have used the Hemlock Stone as a focal for worship but he was sure these were not Druids; they looked more like people who did black magic and worshipped Satan. Whereabouts in time were they? And how were they going to get back?

He was woken from his reverie by Oliver nudging him.

"Look – they are leaving."

So they were; the boys watched the procession wind its way back over the crescent of the hill. At last they were all gone and the boys heaved a sigh of relief.

"Thank goodness, perhaps we can get away from here." Oliver stood up, rubbing his knees. "Ow, my knees really hurt now; I can hardly move."

"Me too." Robin wiped his hands down his legs to rid them of twigs and bits. "Come on, let's get out of here."

The boys both jumped violently as each one was grabbed from behind.

"Not so fast young strangers! You are coming with us."

Chapter 10

The First Meeting

"Let me go – let me - go!" Oliver struggled and kicked out at the man holding him, to no avail. The man's strong arms were wrapped around his body, pinning his arms to his side.

Robin simply stood and then, flexing his whole body, threw off the man holding him with seemingly little effort.

"What the?" Oliver was so startled he stopped his struggling and stared at Robin, wide eyed.

Robin turned to face his assailant. His first thought was that this man looked as if he had stepped right out of The Lord of the Rings. He was young, with shoulder-length dark hair, slightly wavy. He was good looking with dark eyes and a short beard. He was dressed in the kind of gear that would have fitted right into the film.

Robin's mind had a passing thought – had they somehow wondered onto a film set?

Next moment, that idea was shattered when the young man spoke:

"My — such strength - and such strange clothes also." His eyes narrowed. "Could it be that we have stumbled upon the Ring Wearer?" He glanced down at Robin's hands; Robin had one hand over the other, hiding the ring. The man reached forward and moved Robin's hand covering the other. There was the ring in its glory, now glowing its usual red-gold.

"Ah, I see I am right! Thou hast taken me by surprise for I did not expect to come across thee here — but no matter, one can never be quite sure..." he trailed off as if in deep thought. He turned to his companion. "Release the lad."

The other man let go of Oliver so abruptly that he almost lost his balance. He put out a hand to steady him but the boy shook him off.

The man who appeared to be in charge said briskly, "Come with me." And without looking to see if they were following, he turned and stalked off back in amongst the trees. The two boys looked at each other and at the other man, who indicated with his hand to go ahead of him. Realising they had little choice; they followed in the man's footsteps. They walked for some time, having little idea where they were going. Suddenly they came to a cottage; or rather it looked more like a shack, hidden amongst the trees. The man headed into the shack, which appeared to be made of woven twigs.

"Come on in young masters. Come and rest. I have food and drink for thee."

The boys were hesitant; they looked at each other. Robin looked at his ring. It seemed settled; there was no humming and it was shining gold. He felt it was telling him that it was safe here. He nodded and they went inside.

The interior was lit by a torch of fire thrust into a wall somehow; it cast flickering shadows in the small space. There were cosy-looking animal skins on the floor in one corner. The man was sitting on them and indicated they should sit down with him. They did so and moments later, the other man brought them some meat, fruit and water. They took the water and drank; it was fresh and cool. The man nodded. "There is a spring not far away."

"My name is Edric and this is my servant and companion, Orvin. Thou must be wondering what all this is about. What year art thou from?"

Robin thought to himself that, although he had often been asked where he came from he'd never been asked what year he was from!

"2017"

"Hmm, that is a long time. Well, I'm afraid that, as thou art now the Ring Wearer thou hast a task or two to do."

"What sort of tasks?"

At that moment, the man Edric called Orvin came crashing into the hut.

"They are coming master! Quick — we must flee!"

Edric scrambled to his feet hurriedly. He thrust something into Oliver's hand.

"Quick! Thou must go; it's not safe here now. Go back to thine own time — and guard that well." He nodded towards the small leather bag now in Oliver's possession.

"But, how will we get back?" Robin was bewildered. "And what do we have to do?"

"Thou wilt get back by taking off the ring of course. As for thy tasks, the ring will tell thee. Go now, at once, or all will be lost."

"But what about you?"

"Do not worry; all will be well with us. Go!"

Chapter 11

Back to The Present

The boys didn't need telling twice, they ducked out of the hut and ran in the opposite direction to where they could hear shouts coming towards them. They ran and ran until Oliver could barely breathe. Robin was fine; the ring was giving him strength. At last they threw themselves down on a log, Oliver completely unable to run any more.

"Hold onto me, just in case, Ol!" Robin pulled off the ring and put it in his pocket. For a moment, they sat there, completely disorientated and then realised that the mobile was ringing in Oliver's pocket. He pulled it out and swiped the answer button. It was Robin's mum.

"Oliver! Where have you been? I've been sitting here in the car park for half an hour! Where are you?"

The boys got to their feet; they realised they were just inside the woods on the edge of Bramcote Park, not far away from the car park!

"We will be there in just a moment Aunty Carole. Sorry." He shut off the phone and they made their way out of the woods, emerging to bright sunlight. Robin looked at his watch; it said five thirty. They headed towards the car and Robin opened the rear door.

"So there you are! What have you been doing?"

The boys looked at each other – what could they say?

"Sorry mum, we got a bit lost in the woods, took a wrong turning. The mobile never had a signal in there and we were getting worried about getting back."

"Well, never mind, you're here now."

The boys got into the car thankfully. Robin looked back up the road towards the Hemlock Stone, although he couldn't see it from here. He wondered what on earth the ring was going to ask them to do next.

When the car drew into the drive, Robin's mum said:

"Right lads, dinner will be on the table at 6.30. Make sure you are washed and ready please."

"Yes, mum."

"Yes, Aunty Carole."

The boys got out of the car meekly but as soon as they got into Robin's bedroom which they were sharing for the duration of Oliver's stay, they excitedly shut and locked the door and looked at each other.

"Come on then Ol, what did he give you?"

Oliver's hands shook a bit as he loosened the tied leather lace at the top of the soft leather pouch. He turned it upside down so that whatever was inside would fall on the bed. Out slid a gold band, big enough to go round a man's arm. On it were strange markings etched into the gold.

The boys stared at it in silence. Robin plucked his ring out of his pocket and held it next to the band. He looked from one to the other. Then he got a magnifying glass out of a drawer and looked more closely at the ring and then he picked up the band and examined that.

"It looks like the markings on both are the same Ol, see?"

He passed the glass and the ring over and Oliver examined the two items.

"You're right Rob; they are the same. But, however hard I look, I can't see either of them telling us anything."

"I can't either."

"You have to tell me how you got that ring, Rob!"

So Robin related the tale of how he found the ring and how he discovered that it gave him strength.

"But I had no idea it could do anything else – it's amazing, don't you think?"

"I do. I can hardly believe it."

"Yes, it's incredible. But it's not helping us much now is it?"

"No it isn't," said Oliver gloomily, "So - we have a nice matching ring and bracelet set – what are we supposed to do now? Find a girl to wear them, a modern day witch perhaps, who will tell us what to do next?"

Robin laughed. "You've been watching too many fairy tales, mate."

"Listen to you." Oliver grinned. "What I do know is that if we don't get cleaned up ready for dinner, we're going to need more than a magic wand to calm Aunty Carole down."

Chapter 12

The Silver Crystal

The minute the two boys vanished, Edric turned and rushed back to the shack. He muttered and waved and moments later the whole thing vanished, leaving no trace whatsoever.

"Must not leave them any indications," he grinned to his companion. Orvin just nodded silently, readying for more flight.

And in a trice they were off again, almost flying through the woods at great speed, Edric's magic lending them the strength to do so. As they did so, the shouts behind them became less and less until they could hear nothing at all. Edric stopped, panting, and Orvin skidded to a halt beside him.

"Forsooth, I think we have lost them! Now to find out where we are." Edric dipped his hand into his bag and once again brought out the small flat crystal that he had in the cave. Passing his hand over it, he peered into it.

"Ah, we are not far from home. Good news, my friend."

It was indeed, good news to Orvin; he hated the thought of his master in any kind of danger.

Soon the two men came to a large Oak tree, its great girth several times wider than all the other trees around it. As they stood beneath the wide-spread branches, Edric muttered the magic words and, moments later, they were in Edric's palace. Orvin was relieved to be home. However, Edric did not go to relax, he strode off immediately to the cave with the Silver Crystal.

"Watch."

Out of the centre of the Crystal, a wisp of white smoke rose up and flattened out, looking like a large oval mirror before them. Within it, they could see the two boys in Robin's room, studying the amulet and talking together. Edric and Orvin smiled at each other as they listened, amused, to the boys' conversation. They watched them as Robin went to a shelf and took down a small clear case and opening it to reveal something silver, round and flat.

At that point, Edric pointed to the computer in the mirror and began to write in the air with his finger...

Chapter 13

The First Clue

After dinner, Rob and Oliver helped Carole and Roy to clear up the dirty crocks and then they headed back to Robin's room. They said they were going to play on the Wii but really they were hoping to find a clue as to what the next step of their adventure was to be.

But, it didn't matter how much they examined the two items, rubbed them or wore them, nothing happened.

"Oh, I can't be bothered with this Rob. Let's watch a film."

"Oh ok, what do you fancy?"

"I think I'd like to watch 'Prince Caspian', you've got it haven't you?"

"Of course"

Rob and Oliver put the ring and the amulet down on the computer table and Rob went to get the DVD while Oliver put the television on. When Robin turned round from the DVD shelves, he suddenly grabbed his cousin's arm.

Oliver looked to where Rob was pointing – at the computer. Words were appearing on the screen.

"But – but that's not possible – it's not even switched on!" Oliver whispered.

The DVD forgotten, the boys watched, fascinated, as the words appeared gradually. The writing was curly, old fashioned. When it stopped, there were just two lines of curious writing on the screen:

Depedale is where you must go to ask

A humble hermit for his staff

"Eh? What can that mean?" Oliver was astounded. "And where on earth is Depedale? I've never heard of it."

"Nor me. Shall we go and ask dad? Bet he knows."

"No, he will want to know why we want to know. Put the computer on and type in 'Depedale' and see what comes up."

"Good idea."

There was a silence from the boys while they waited impatiently for the computer to log on. At last it was ready and Robin googled 'Depedale'.

"Hey, look Oliver – it says it's the old name for Dale Abbey! And fancy, it's the place where Alan-a-Dale of Robin Hood fame was married. Oh, and look here – it says that a baker from Derby went to live in Depedale after seeing a vision of the Virgin Mary and she told him to devote his life to prayer. He became a hermit and lived in a cave in Depedale. Later, an order of monks established an Abbey there because it was reputed to be a holy place."

"In that case, it looks like we have to pay a visit to Dale Abbey then. But how would we get this hermit to give us his staff? We have to have something to give to him in exchange. He won't want money; in any case we wouldn't have the right money to give him for that time. What shall we do?"

"We will think about it – shall we watch the film now? Perhaps an idea will come. Shall we plan to go on a bike ride there tomorrow?"

"Yes to both; we will watch the film and plan our trip to Dale Abbey."

Later, as the boys tried to sleep, they found it very difficult because they were excited about the next step of their adventures.

Chapter 14

Back into History

The next day was Easter Sunday, which meant that church would be tempered by a pocketful of mini eggs. The boys sucked them secretly as they sat in the church. Robin's mum was well aware of it but she let it go; after all, Easter only happened once a year. As long as they didn't eat too much chocolate and spoil their dinner or worse, be sick, she was fine with it. The boys found it difficult to concentrate on the service; they were so taken up with thoughts of their future visit to Dale Abbey and what might occur there.

Dinner was good; lovely roast beef, Yorkshire puddings, roast potatoes and vegetables. It was Robin's and Oliver's favourite meal and they ate with relish.

"So, what do you lads have planned for this afternoon?" Robin's dad wanted to know.

"We were thinking of taking a bike ride."

"Oh well, that will be good for you. Where do you think you might go? At least the roads will be fairly quiet today, it being Sunday."

"Well, we were thinking of Dale Abbey. It's been a long time since we've been there."

"Dale Abbey eh? Well, that will certainly test your stamina! Make sure you take your Ventolin Robin."

"Yes dad, I'll be fine. What will you and mum do while we are gone?"

"Oh, I'm sure we will find something."

"Sleep I expect." Robin laughed. His dad laughed too.

"Cheeky, but you're probably right."

"Would you like another picnic then - or just a few snacks to keep you going?"

"What do you think OI?"

"Oh, a picnic please — I love your picnics Aunty Carole!"

"Alright then, I will make you some food to take with you."

The boys ran off to get changed and collect the ring and the amulet. When they came down, the food was packed and ready.

"Thanks so much mum – you're wonderful."

"Flattery will get you anywhere." Carol laughed.

The boys packed their bags hastily. As they went towards the front door, Robin saw a bag that his mum had put ready for a charity collection. A fleecy blanket was at the top. He looked at it and on impulse, pulled it out of the bag, rolled it as small as it would go and stuffed it in his bag.

Oliver had already gone out of the house, helmet on, and had his leg over Robin's dad's bike, which he borrowed when he was visiting.

"Come on Rob – what are you doing?" he shouted.

Robin appeared in the doorway, backpack on and doing his helmet up as he came. He grabbed his bike and they were off.

Dale Abbey was in the opposite direction to the Hemlock Stone; and it was mostly uphill. It was quite a hard ride, but they kept stopping to rest and at times walked. When the road dipped again, they rode. It took them quite a while to get there; in a car it would have taken only about fifteen minutes or so. It was a beautiful day; daffodils bobbed in the grass verges and the sky was very blue and lovely. They were able to ride into the village as it was reasonably flat there and then they turned left and down towards the field where one could gain entry into the ruins of the abbey and also, to the right, the woods where the hermit's cave could be found.

The boys climbed over the stile into the field; they wanted to look at the large archway that was all that remained of the once great abbey, although the houses nearest to the ruins had bits of the abbey walls built into them and other houses in the village were built of the stones taken from it. The arch was on farmland, but visitors were allowed to go and look. The two lads gazed at the arch towering above them, still an awesome sight standing in its isolated state.

"I wish I could see what it was once like," Oliver said as they looked at the sunlight glinting on the stones.

"Yes me too. I bet it was quite something."

"Strange to have a huge Abbey like that in the middle of nowhere."

"Well, the monks came here because it was reputed to be a holy place, once news got around of the hermit's vision."

Oliver stood, as if in thought for a few minutes.

"Yes. Well, let's get down to business! What shall we do, find the path to the hermit's cave first?"

"Yes, it's over there. If we get on the path we stand a better chance of not getting lost."

There was a signpost that said 'To Hermit's Cave'. There were many nettles and thistles in the field so they needed to tread carefully. Once on the beginning of the path, Robin took out his ring and Oliver put on the amulet.

"How can we be sure we will go back to the right time?" Oliver wondered.

"I feel that we should say the clue as I put on the ring."

"Right, let's do that. Can you remember it?"

Robin took a scrap of paper from his pocket. "I wrote it down, just in case."

"Good thinking."

The boys linked their little fingers (they felt silly holding hands) and chanted the two lines together:

"Depedale is where you must ask, a humble hermit for his staff."

Robin slid his ring on while they were chanting the lines. They shut their eyes. Robin opened his eyes and nudged Oliver. "Look!"

They looked in the direction he was pointing, and there before them was a magnificent abbey, standing in grounds that were beautiful and well kept, with other buildings around, which were obviously the monks' living areas. They were stunned. The vision, however, faded away and the abbey disappeared altogether. There were no buildings, no ruined arch, nothing, just an expanse of wild land.

"Well, mate, looks like the ring gave you your wish to see the abbey. Now we are further back in time. We have to see to our task."

The boys turned in the direction they knew they had to go, but before they had gone many steps, they heard a sudden 'swoosh' and an arrow thunked into a tree just in front of them.

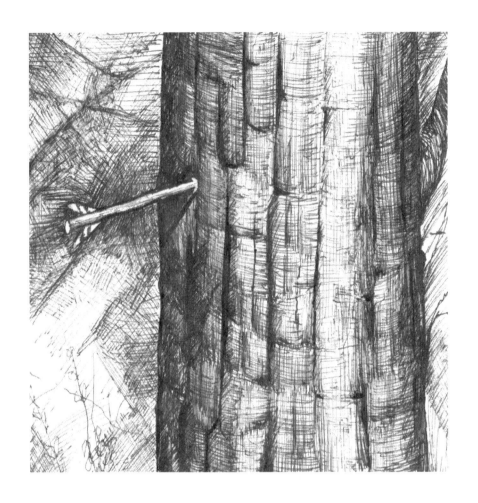

Chapter 15

Sir Ralf

"Run!" Robin heard Oliver shout and, without stopping to think he obeyed. They could hear the sound of horses' hooves pounding behind them. Somewhere in Robin's mind he knew they didn't have a chance of getting away, especially as the modern-day path through the trees was not there and running was difficult. Before they got far, an arrow thumped into another tree, this time only just above their heads. It brought them up short as they heard a voice shout:

"Stop there or the next arrow will not be in a tree."

The boys froze. Robin stole a look at his ring. He was surprised that it was its usual red-gold colour; he realised in a moment that they were not in danger. He relaxed. He whispered to Oliver:

"The ring says it's ok. But hide the amulet up your sleeve; we don't want it discovered."

Oliver obeyed immediately, shoving the amulet up his arm in a swift movement and pulling his sleeve over it.

The boys turned round to see three men striding towards them. The one in the front was obviously in charge. There was a fourth man standing further back with the horses.

"Who art thou? And what doest thou trespassing on my hunting land?"

Robin drew in his breath; he knew who this man was! He nudged Oliver and then bowed to the man, Oliver follow suit.

"Sir Ralph, I humbly beg your forgiveness my lord."

Ralph FitzGeremund looked startled. He was a man of average build and height, with dark red hair and a trim beard, both with distinctive flecks of grey, showing he was middle aged. There was an air about him that commanded respect. He strode closer to the boys.

"Thou knowest me?" His voice had an attractive accent; indeed, he was from Normandy. Robin had read that he owned a vast area of land, which, in modern days would encompass Ockbrook, Borrowash, Long Eaton and surrounding villages. He was a man of great power in his time.

"I, er, your reputation has travelled far sir. I have heard that you are a great man and a much respected lord. My friend and I are, um, travellers sir."

"I note that thy raiments are strange and thou speakest strangely, although I can understand thee. From whence dost thou come?"

"It is difficult to explain my lord, but we have come a very long way. We are on an errand, sir."

"An errand? What is that?"

"Well, you could say it is a quest, sir. We have come to seek a favour from the hermit who resides in these woods."

"A hermit? I know of no such person residing on my land."

"His fame has spread far and wide my lord; we have been sent to find him to hear words of wisdom and faith from him."

'*My goodness Robin my lad, but you're good.*'he thought to himself.

"Well then, we must find this particularly astounding person mustn't we? Lead the way young sirs!"

Chapter 16

The Hermit

Finding the way wasn't easy. When Robin had been before, there had been a well-marked path, made wide and clear by the many walkers who had gone before. Now, so many hundreds of years before, the whole area was vastly different. There was no wide path, just a faint track which had probably been made by the hermit himself as he walked the area. Robin just hoped they were going in the right general direction as he tried to remember it. It was tough going, and he was very aware of the three men who were with them; the fourth man had remained behind with the horses.

As it turned out, it wasn't very far, for which the boys were thankful. They spotted wisps of smoke winding their way upwards and came upon the hermit himself, sitting by his meagre fire, outside his cave.

The cave was a rough affair; it was not a natural one. It had been carved out of the sandstone by the hermit himself and had a doorway and a 'window' either side.

Robin was not sure what to expect a hermit to look like; he'd had some kind of idea that he would be an imposing figure with long white hair and a long beard, with long flowing clothes, something like Gandalf or Dumbledore. This man didn't much resemble them; he looked very poor indeed, painfully thin and wearing rough and ragged clothes. He looked much older than Sir Ralph; his remaining hair was iron-grey, straggly and unkempt. He stood up upon seeing his visitors and he was rather stooped. He sort of bowed to Sir Ralph, but then looked at the boys with astonishment and puzzlement. He looked enquiringly back at the knight that stood before him.

"My good man, what art thou doing here, living like this on my land?" Sir Ralph spoke quietly and pleasantly, not wanting to frighten him.

"Some years ago I dreamed a dream in which the Virgin Mary appeared to me and told me to come and live in Depedale and devote my life to prayer. So I left my work in Derby and came here. I made myself this dwelling out of the stone side and have lived here since; praying for the world and my fellow beings."

"My dear fellow, look at thee; thou art so thin and poor. What dost thou eat?"

"I eat what I findest on the ground and on the trees. Sometimes a kind person in the village gives me some bread."

"Well, I can't have you living here like this!"

The poor man fell on his knees. "Oh, please don't turn me out my lord; I am only doing My Lady's wishes."

"I have no intention of turning thee out. I am impressed that a man should give up everything to devote himself to prayer but I can't have thee starving to death like this. In future thou will receive a tithe from my mill in Borrowash; it will mean you can buy food and other things to keep you warm in the winters. I'm surprised thou hast survived this long. "

"When thou doest the Will of the Lord, He looks after thee."

"So it seems! Well, I am also looking after thee now."

"I think that may be the same thing My Lord. But I am very grateful to thee, sir."

"Very well. Now, I must away. These are two young strangers who have travelled far to see thee."

"To see me? But why?"

Robin looked briefly at Oliver and then stepped forward.

"We have come to learn from you and to get your help in something we seek."

"I am sure that I have nothing that I can help thee with, but thou art welcome to my humble abode."

Robin turned to Sir Ralph and bowed low to him. "Thank you, My Lord; my friend and I are very grateful to you and humbled at the privilege of meeting you sir."

"I wish thee well in thy quest."

"Thank you." Robin bowed again, as did Oliver. They watched Sir Ralph and his servants stride away through the trees. Then they turned towards the old man watching them curiously. Robin really did not know how he was going to ask this poor creature for anything.

Chapter 17

Mission Accomplished

Oliver was the first to get things moving. He pulled his backpack down and set it on the ground.

"Well sir, we have travelled a long way and we are hungry. Why don't we eat our food together and then discuss what we have come for?"

"Good idea Oliver," Robin followed suit and shrugged his bag off his back. The hermit, who said his name was John*, watched with interest as the boys unpacked their picnic.

"What strange food thou hast, young sirs; I've never seen the like of it!"

"But you will like it though. Try a sandwich." Oliver handed a ham sandwich to the man, who looked at it suspiciously.

*Not the Hermit's actual name as far as I know

"It is alright, it is meat inside it. It's quite safe." Oliver took a bite of his own sandwich to prove his point. John tentatively bit into his one and, after hesitating a moment, savouring the flavours, hastily ate the rest as if he thought it would be taken away again. Oliver laughed and gave him more which went the same way, very quickly. The boys had pork pies, sausage rolls, boiled eggs as well as the sandwiches, all of which were eaten with enthusiasm by John.

"If you are not used to eating much, I wouldn't eat too much now. We will leave you some for tomorrow." Robin was wise enough to know that the strange food might not sit very well in the hermit's stomach! Fortunately, John was sensible enough to realise this and he allowed Robin to leave some food wrapped up in the strange bags and Robin offered to put it in the cave. John nodded.

"Thank you young sir; you will see some shelves on which to put it."

Robin entered the cave, which was unlit except for the light filtering in from outside. There were indeed shelves cut into the sandstone and there were niches with tallow candles for night times. Robin had an ulterior motive for wanting to go into the cave; he wanted to see if the hermit did indeed have a staff, for it was certainly not outside. In a moment he found what he sought; propped up against a corner was a staff. Robin went over to it and ran his finger along it. It answered him with a faint tingle in his hand; he had no doubt this was the item they were after. Now, the tricky part was how to get it. There was no way he was going to steal it, it was wrong to steal and anyway they could not steal from a man who had so little. Somehow, he had to think of a way. He went back outside.

"All on the shelf safely now." He sat down next to John and then moved away a little as if he wanted to look at his face. Really, it was because the man smelt rather! "Please tell us more about the experience you had."

As the man talked, Robin wracked his brains as to how he could ask for the staff; he wished they had something they could offer in its place.

The light was beginning to fade and Robin felt they needed to get back through the woods before it got dark; in any case, his parents would be worried if they got home too late. He stood up.

"I think we should be going now as it is getting dark. I am worried about going through the woods not being able to see properly."

John stood up too, as did Oliver.

"Wait there, young masters." Oliver and Robin looked at each other while John made his way into the cave. Could it be...?

John reappeared, the staff in his hand.

"I will guide thee back through the woods, it's the least I can do after all that wonderful food thou hast given me and thy attentive listening ears."

The boys followed John as he walked confidently through the trees, using his staff to clear his path.

Along the way, Oliver's sharp eyes found another stout stick lying on the ground and picked it up. It was about the same size as the hermit's staff. Olli walked along, using it the same way as the hermit. He winked at Robin.

When they got to the point where the boys had met Sir Ralph, they stopped. Oliver turned to John.

"I don't suppose you would be willing to give us something to take back home to our people, to show them we have seen you and spoken to you?"

"I would willingly, but, as thou hast seen, I have nothing."

"Please, could we have your staff? I found this along the way and you could use it instead."

John looked at his staff, rather surprised at such a request.

"But how will this prove thou hast seen me? It is just an ordinary piece of wood."

"No, it's not. It has been rubbed smooth by your hands and we can feel that it has the power of prayer in it. Our people will be able to feel it when they touch it." Robin was choosing his words carefully.

"Will they?" John was astonished.

"Yes. And, if you take this one instead, it will become like that one, so that if anyone like us comes along again, it will be something you can give them."

"How strange," the man declared. "Yes, take the staff with my blessings."

He handed it to Oliver, who took it with reverence. Robin suddenly thought of the blanket he had stuffed into his bag before they left home. He brought it out now and gave it to the man.

"It's a blanket; it will help keep you warm."

John stroked the fleecy material in wonder.

"Such strange food, now strange cloth, I've never seen the like."

"Um... it was made in a country far away, my father traded for it. We would like you to have it to thank you for your goodwill towards us."

"In that case, I thank thee, young sirs. Today has been a wonderful day. I must go and pray my thanks to My Lady."

He took the new staff gravely from Oliver, bowed slightly to the boys and stepped back towards the woods. They watched him for a few moments until he had disappeared through the trees.

Chapter 18

Home Again

The boys linked fingers as before and Robin took off his ring. Moments later, they were back on the entrance to the wide path into the woods, the ruined arch sitting in the field in their line of vision.

They waited for a few moments for their heads to clear and then set off back to where they had left their bikes. It didn't seem so late here as it had in the woods with the hermit. Robin checked his watch and it was only quarter to seven. It had felt much later than that, but he remembered about the last time they went on a trip with the ring it had been night time at the Hemlock Stone but still daytime when they got back. It was disorientating but they were getting used to it.

The staff was something of a trial on the way home; it was so long that it was very awkward. In the end, Oliver found some lengths of string in his bag (he always had useful things) and tied it along his crossbar. The end stuck out behind him but at least he could cope with that.

The ride home was much easier because it was mostly downhill and it took them far less time to do it.

"Oh, there you are, boys." Carol greeted them cheerfully when they came in. "We were just wondering where you had got to. Have you had a good day?"

"Yes, it's been a very interesting day, thank you, mum. Is there anything to eat?" he asked hopefully.

"What, after all that food I packed up for you, you want more?" Carol looked at them, eyes wide as if in surprise.

The boys were indeed hungry, for they had given most of their food to the hermit but they couldn't tell her that could they?

"Well mum, you know what they say about growing boys and fresh air, don't you? We're starving."

Carol laughed. "Oh ok then! I have a pizza you can have; I'll just pop it in the oven."

The boys went to put their bikes in the garage and then came in, Oliver carrying the staff. Carol looked at him.

"Whatever have you got there, Oliver?"

"It's a hermit's staff, Aunty Carol; we got it from near the hermit's cave."

"Oh, you boys and your imaginations! I suppose you're going to keep it to pretend you're adventurers or wizards or something."

"Something like that, Aunty!" Oliver grinned at her and went off upstairs carrying the precious staff. Robin followed.

They didn't need to hide the staff so they leaned it up in a corner of the bedroom. They changed their jogger bottoms, knowing they would be dirty as they'd sat on the ground with the hermit, washed their hands and thundered back down the stairs for the pizza, which now smelled very inviting.

Later, when they were back in Robin's bedroom, they looked up the information again about the hermit in Depedale.

"That's funny," remarked Oliver.

"What is?"

"Well, it says here that Ralph FitzGeremund found the hermit on his land after seeing smoke rising from the fire. It says nothing about him being guided to the hermit by a pair of young time-travellers."

The boys laughed.

"And I don't suppose that, if the blanket was ever found in the cave, that anyone thought it had actually been used by the hermit himself."

"Now that would indeed be a puzzle for archaeologists! Especially if they found it before fleecy blankets had been invented."

Chapter 19

Alton Towers

The lads slept soundly that night; they'd had a lot of fresh air and exercise that day. They knew they would not be able to go adventuring again the next day because Robin's parents were going to take them to Alton Towers. It was Easter bank holiday Monday and Robin's dad had the day off work. The boys couldn't really refuse to go out with them as they had planned the day with the boys in mind. In any case, Robin and Oliver loved Alton Towers!

When they got up in the morning, there, on the computer screen was another message:

Neath clouds that are below the skye

Is where the magical sphere doth lye

"Wow Robin – look at that! I forgot we left the ring and amulet by the computer again."

Robin came over to look at the screen.

"That looks exciting doesn't it? A magical sphere eh? I can't help wondering what all this is about really."

"And what could it mean about clouds that are below the sky?" wondered Oliver.

"I dunno, we can think about it while we are out. We know we can't do anything about it today anyway."

"We had better put the ring and the amulet away somewhere; we don't want someone spotting them, the window cleaner or something."

"No, too true."

The boys tucked the two items into the leather pouch and buried them deep in a drawer. Then they collected their things and went down for breakfast.

They had a great day at Alton Towers; it was very busy there, it being a bank holiday but, as the boys queued to go on the rides they didn't care. They enjoyed getting wet on the log flume and being terrified on other rides. Robin's parents left them to it, just checking in with them now and then on the mobile phone. They had money to buy food and they bought hot dogs, burgers, drank pop and had ice creams. They should have felt thoroughly sick what with the terrible food and the rides flinging them around but they didn't.

Robin's parents went on some of the rides, the rather less terrifying ones and also spent some time strolling around the Pagoda gardens where it was comparatively peaceful.

At one point the boys wandered around the ruined building that gave Alton Towers its name; it had once been a great house and this adventure playground was on what was once the estate.

Robin always had a 'thing' for ruined places; he just loved to imagine what it would have been like years ago when people lived in them. Alton Towers was quite a mysterious place really. But the mystery was dispelled in the noise and bustle of the adventure land.

It took some time to get away from the car park when it was time to go. There were fields full of cars and they were all leaving at once.

As Robin sat in the back of the car idly watching the scenery go by, his mind drifted back to the clue that had been on the computer that morning. Something seemed to click into place — 'clouds that are below the sky' — of course! He nudged Oliver and whispered:

"I have the answer — the clue means Stoney Clouds. 'Clouds that are below the sky' — Stoney Clouds."

"My gosh, Rob, you're right! Next stop — Stoney Clouds."

Chapter 20

Stoney Clouds

The next day found the boys wending their way up to Stoney Clouds, the usual backpacks on stuffed with food and water. Oliver carried the staff and was wearing the amulet up his sleeve. He was always anxious about it as it was too big for him really, so he pushed it up as high as it would go in the hope he would not lose it.

It was another beautiful day and the boys were looking forward to their next adventure. They made their way up past the lovely old church and through the gate at the top of the lane which led into the area the locals called Stoney Clouds. The original name for the place was 'Stoney Cluds', which means 'stony fields'.

They followed the path and went past the top of 'Cardboard Hill' where the local children and young at heart slid down the hill on toboggans and trays during snowy times and came round to the spot the boys always called 'The Lookout'. It was the point of land that was above the huge boulders which gave the area its name as they looked like huge stony clouds; smooth looking brown rocks that protruded from the hillside. From here they could look across the motorway at Stanton Ironworks and the land in that area. Beneath them, at the bottom of the slopes there was a golf course.

The boys sat for a while on the seat and watched the vehicles travelling along the motorway. By the time they had seen their third 'Eddie Stobart' lorry, they decided it was time to do something!

Robin took out the piece of paper on which he had written the latest clue and looked at it thoughtfully.

"You know, Ol, it says 'Neath clouds that are below the sky.' I think that means we should be down there." He pointed down to the golf course. "Because 'neath' is an old fashioned word for 'beneath'."

"I think you're right Rob," agreed Oliver and so they got up to make their way down the rocky face, knowing there were pathways between the trees. It was trickier than going down Cardboard Hill, but they were on an adventure after all. And, keeping in the trees, they were less likely to be seen.

When they finally got down to the level of the golf course, they could see it could be complicated as there were several people playing golf because it was a lovely day. They wouldn't be able to just disappear in front of these people!

"What shall we do Rob?"

"Let's go back among trees and do it there and hopefully we won't be seen."

Thus agreed, they moved back into the cover of the trees and then Oliver held onto Robin's shoulder and together they chanted the lines as he put on the ring. As they did so they saw the motorway, above them now, fade away. They looked around them and there was no sign of Stanton Ironworks or any other familiar landmark. They walked out into the open, which was now rough ground and not a smooth and sleek golf course.

They turned towards their left, which was in the direction the motorway had been. Here they could see clearly the stony 'clouds' that some say gives the area its name, usually only seen from the motorway. In summer they were even harder to see, hidden as they were by all the leaves on the trees that grew there. Now, there were no trees, just a huge, rocky cliff that towered above them. They couldn't believe how different it looked! As they walked around the cliff, they spotted a dark crevice, hidden behind a low rock – could it be a cave? They walked up to it and peered in; it looked dark and creepy.

"I don't think I want to go in there you know." Robin was not at all happy at the thought; he hated the dark and the thought of being underground.

"Nor me really, mate. Let's..." At that moment, a loud crash of thunder made them jump; they had not noticed the sky darken rapidly because they were so interested in their different surroundings. All at once, the sky opened and the rain pelted down so thick and fast that the boys immediately ran into the cave without thinking. They stood just inside, watching the rain coming down like a sheet.

"Gosh, just look at that! I never noticed the storm coming, did you Ol?"

"Not at all mate. I think Somebody or Something sent that storm to make us come in here!"

"Give us a push you mean - because we weren't going to come in?"

"That's exactly what I mean."

Robin let out a long sigh. He turned around and looked towards the blackness at the rear of the cave. He braced his shoulders.

"Right - in that case, I guess we'd better get on with it."

Rather reluctantly, the boys walked towards the back of the cave, where they found, not entirely to their surprise, a tunnel. Gingerly, they walked on and were soon swallowed up by the blackness.

Chapter 21

The Golden Sphere

As the boys rounded a bend, feeling their way along the rocky walls, a light suddenly flared above them. They looked up in surprise, to see that the light was actually coming from the hermit's staff, carried by Oliver.

"Oh cool!" Exclaimed Oliver.

"Well, fancy that. I felt a tingle when I touched it in the hermit's cave but I'd no idea it could do something like that. I'm glad though, I hate this darkness," said Robin.

"Me too," agreed Oliver fervently. He shivered. "It's cold in here too, isn't it? I wonder how far we will have to go down here."

"Dunno." Robin really didn't want to talk; he could feel the familiar feeling of panic rising that he always got when in underground places. The boys walked on in silence, keeping an eye on their feet as they walked along the uneven ground.

Suddenly, the passage opened out into a wide space. As Oliver shone the staff-light around them they could see stalagmites and stalactites creating a wonderful and mysterious landscape. The walls glittered as the light flickered on the different layers of stones that lined the cave. In spite of his fear, Robin was fascinated at the scene before him; he had never seen anything quite so beautiful. As the boys explored the cave, dipping their fingers in the clear pools of water that mirrored the columns of rock that had formed over thousands of years, they quite forgot where they were.

As they moved around, looking at everything, Robin suddenly spotted something else that glittered in the torchlight and his heart jumped – could it be the magic sphere in the clue? He inched nearer to the object, which appeared to be sitting in a pool of water.

"Oliver - come over here – shine the light there – look."

Oliver came over and positioned the staff so that they could see more clearly the beautiful round gold object sitting on – sitting on? – the water. On closer inspection, they could see it was actually resting on a submerged stalagmite, the top of which just reached the surface of the pool. It was a long way over – how were they going to get it?

"If I give you a leg up, can you reach over to it?" Oliver said to Robin

"It would probably be better if I lifted you up – I'm strong with the ring, remember?"

"Oh yes. Okay then, let's try it."

Oliver propped the staff up against the wall, positioned so it illuminated the area he was going to try to reach. Robin crouched down, and, clasping his hands around Oliver's lower legs, he lifted him up carefully, staggering slightly until he got used to the weight. Gradually, he lifted Oliver higher until he could bend over the edge of the pool, which was higher than his waist height. He stretched out his hand; it was centimetres away from the ball.

"A bit higher, Rob, if you can," he panted, and, as Rob gave him a little more leverage, his fingers came into contact with the ball. Immediately, he gave a yowl and, startled, Robin let him slip a bit and his chest got wet in the pool. It was not deep and his hand plunged into the water to steady himself.

"Wassup, wassup?" panted Robin as he had the presence of mind to grab Oliver's legs again.

"It gave me an electric shock! It won't let me pick it up."

"Come on down then, we will have to rethink this one." Robin let Oliver down carefully. Oliver looked at his front ruefully.

"I might as well have stayed out in that rain!"

"I'm sorry I dropped you, mate, but you gave me a fright, yelling like that."

"I couldn't help it – it hurt!" Oliver looked at his hand but it seemed ok. "I think it's because it has to be you that gets it."

"Do you reckon? Are you going to be able to lift me that far?"

"Well, I'll have to try won't I?"

The boys repositioned themselves; this time Oliver put his hands together and Robin stepped a foot onto them. He helped by hauling himself up with his hands until he could bend over the edge of the pool. He stretched out his hand, but, try as he might, he just could not reach it; Oliver could not lift him up high enough.

"Put me down Ol, we will have to try something else. Oh, hang on – can you manage to give me the amulet?"

"I think so. Just see if you can hold on because I'll have to let you go for a moment."

Robin held onto the edge of the pool for dear life, his nose very close to the water. Then he felt the reassuring grip on his lower legs again and he reached down to take the amulet that Oliver was holding up to him. He just managed to get it and then he stretched out once again towards the ball, holding the amulet as far out as he could. As if by magic, the ball almost jumped into the middle of the amulet.

"Got it!"

Oliver let Robin down thankfully and when he was back on his feet, both the boys looked carefully at the golden ball, still in the centre of the amulet. It was a bit bigger than a tennis ball and had the same curious markings on it that the ring and the amulet had. They looked at each other, eyes shining – they had their third magic item!

"Let's get out of here." Oliver reached for the staff. As he picked it up, he caught sight of the ring on Robin's finger. Once again, it was gleaming bright red.

Chapter 22

A Frightening Run

At that same moment, as the boys gazed at the glowing ring, they heard a noise – a deep, nasal sort of sound, followed by a deep sigh. It actually sounded like something – a very large something – was sleeping somewhere nearby. The boys gazed around fearfully,

Oliver moving the staff-light around cautiously. What could it be?

The light caught something that shone a sort of greenish-gold colour and Oliver moved the light carefully along the form lying on the floor at the back of the cave. To their absolute amazement it was –

"A dragon?" whispered Oliver in wonder.

"Can't be – whoever heard of a dragon in Sandiacre? That's stupid." whispered back Robin. They stood and gazed at the huge creature and, as they looked, they heard its breathing hesitate and change – and then a golden eye appeared. The boys started back into the shadows, the staff-light dimmed all on its own.

"It's waking up! What shall we do?"

"Will we have to kill it?" Oliver said.

"No way – what do we have to kill it with? Anyway, I don't want to kill it – it's amazing! It's beautiful – perhaps it's the last dragon in the country - I am not going to kill the last dragon. But we have to get out of here quickly before it realises we are here."

"Um…I think we may be too late…" Robin looked to where Oliver was standing fearfully watching the great creature as it looked around, still lying on its haunches.

The boys backed away, very carefully, all the time watching the creature as it became more aware of their presence. They were making good headway in putting more space between them and the dragon, for a dragon it undoubtedly was, when it suddenly got up and came towards them. They gave a yell and ran for it. They ran as fast as they could but they knew the dragon was not far behind. It hiccupped a flame at them and they pressed themselves to the wall of the tunnel and it never touched them. Obviously, this dragon was out of practise as far as his fire was concerned. The boys kept going until Oliver suddenly tripped over and fell. Robin stopped.

"No, don't stop, Robin – I've twisted my ankle I think!" gasped Oliver. "You must get away – save yourself. I will try to keep it interested so you can get away."

"No way, mate!" In one movement, Robin bent over and swept up his cousin, and ran on with him. It was amazing; he seemed to carry Oliver's weight with no more trouble than he would have carrying a bag and his running suddenly became as though he was Superman or something, the walls of the tunnel were flying past him quick as lightning.

It took a very short space of time before they reached the entrance cave. They could hear the dragon coming behind them; even that couldn't outrun Robin, although it was getting closer. Robin ran right out of the cave, dumped Oliver unceremoniously on the ground and pulled off his ring.

The cave closed behind them, the trees reappeared, the motorway was there and they were sitting on the golf course, surprising a dog who was sniffing around near the line of trees and he ran off, yelping, his tail between his legs.

The boys fell on their backs, arms flung out and gazing up at the sky, which was bright and clear.

"Phew – that was CLOSE!" Robin lay, panting.

"Wow, that was *wicked* – you were awesome! I can't believe you picked me up and ran like that – how did you do it?"

"It was the ring of course. It gives me the strength I need when I call upon it. There was no other way we could have got out of there."

"I am so grateful – I didn't fancy becoming a dragon's dinner really."

"Well, I can't believe there was a dragon in there. Whoever heard of dragons around here? Don't they belong in another time and place, with knights and maidens in distress and stuff?"

"Well, it was certainly another time. And I was in distress alright – well at least I would have been if the dragon had got me!"

"Well, that's a new slant on the dragon thing." Robin grinned. "Maybe I should call you Maid Marion or Princess Fiona or something."

"Don't you dare!" Oliver rolled over and punched Robin lightly in the chest. Next moment they were rolling around on the grass play-fighting. Then they stopped and sat up.

"How's your ankle Ol?"

"I dunno; it hurts rather."

Robin helped Oliver to get up and he stood carefully on his foot.

"It's not too bad; I think I can manage."

"Well, you have a staff to help you."

"That's true. I say Rob – we forgot something!"

"What? Have we left something behind?" Robin looked worried.

"No – we haven't eaten our food – I'm starving!"

Chapter 23

A Quiet Period and Another Clue

As it turned out, Oliver's ankle was too painful to walk on. Robin called his mum and asked if she could bring the car up to the golf club. He put on the ring and then he carried his cousin piggy-back style across the golf course to the clubhouse and out through the gate to the lane whilst Oliver hung onto all the bags and things. At least the bags were not heavy as they had now eaten all their food. They sat on the grass verge to await Carole.

She was alarmed that Oliver's ankle was so painful and swollen. She took him to Accident and Emergancy where they sat for ages waiting to be seen. Rob insisted on going with them. It turned out to be a sprain and he was told to rest it up for a couple of days with ice packs.

This meant there were going to be no adventures for the lads for the next few days. They amused themselves in and around the house, playing computer games and watching films.

The lads were getting worried because Oliver was going home on Sunday; his parents were coming to pick him up. And they still had some more adventuring to do – didn't they? However, it didn't matter how much they left the amulet and ring by the computer, nothing showed. They swallowed their disappointment and just got on with their activities, giving the boy's ankle time to heal. To further keep them in, it rained in true English weather style, so there was no way they wanted to be out anyway.

By Thursday Oliver said his ankle was feeling better, although his foot was all shades of purple. With the stoicism of a boy, he insisted that by the next day it would be just fine. Carole said she would see... They knew what that meant!

As it happened, Oliver was not all that disappointed to be able to give his foot another day's rest. He and Rob never got fed up with the things they did; they played a rousing game of Monopoly and an even more vicious game of 'Sorry'! Although they loved their video games, they loved the old board games too. They even played a very challenging game of tiddly-winks and marbles! Robin's cat got involved in the game, which they played in the sitting room as there was a good expanse of floor to roll the marbles on. There were groans and shouts of 'gerrof' and helpless laughter as they watched the cat chasing the marbles and patting them about, completely ruining the game but providing them with much entertainment.

"Ok, that's enough now. Put the marbles away boys. Your dad will be home soon and it will be teatime."

Rob and Oliver gathered up the marbles and Rob picked up the other games and went to take them upstairs to put them away.

Oliver put the television on. He thought that Rob was taking a long time to come down again and wondered what he was doing.

When Robin came down, he closed the door firmly behind him and said in a low voice:

"There's been another clue!"

Oliver looked at him joyfully.

"What is it?"

Rob took out a paper from his pocket, looked around him as if he thought someone was trying to listen and then quietly read the clue out.

"The Giant's plaything is his throne,

And where he will come into his own."

"The Giant's plaything – what's that?" Oliver frowned.

"The only thing I can think of is the Hemlock Stone – legend says a giant threw it there."

Oliver looked at his cousin thoughtfully.

"Then it looks like we have to go back to where we started – the Hemlock Stone."

Chapter 24

The Hemlock Stone

"It is our last day together mum, please do let us go!"

It was Saturday and the boys were at the table, eating rather a late breakfast.

Carol wasn't at all sure that she should let the boys go out; she was worried about Oliver's foot.

"Where are you going to go? You will have to be very careful."

"We would like to go back to Bramcote Park."

"But what can you do there? Oliver certainly can't go in the woods again with his foot."

"No, we won't go into the woods. We want to go up to the Hemlock Stone. We've heard, that is, we believe, there may be some kind of show going on up there. We can just take a waterproof sheet and sit and watch and eat a picnic."

"What do you think Roy?" Carol appealed to Robin's dad. He looked at the boys' eager faces.

"Oh, I think it will be okay for a couple of hours. We can drop them off there and go do the shopping, then fetch them after."

"Oh ok then. I'll pack you a picnic; I suppose it would be a shame to waste your last day together indoors. And it looks like it's going to be a nice day."

"Thanks, Mum – thanks, Dad." Robin got up and hugged his mum and clapped his hand on his dad's shoulder.

Later that day they were all packed and in the car ready to go. Robin couldn't help his heart thumping – what was going to happen at the Hemlock Stone? The last time they were there had been frightening really, with Edric and Orvin being chased by those men; he hoped they had got away. He wondered who they would meet on their trip this time – and was this the end of their adventures?

It took a very short time to get to the park. The boys were dropped off at the point nearest to where they could cross the road to the Hemlock Stone. Oliver carried the staff and had the amulet up his sleeve. Robin had the golden ball in his pocket and, of course, the ring. They had the inevitable back-packs with their picnics in and they waved Robin's parents off cheerfully.

Then they made their way through to the crossing, over the road and onto the path that led to the Hemlock Stone. Oliver said little, but Robin guessed that his ankle was still hurting him. It was just as well they hadn't far to go. They made their way up to the stone slowly. Oliver leaned heavily on the staff as he hobbled along.

"I hope we can find a moment when there's no one around." Robin commented as they walked along.

"Well, it doesn't take long does it? I'm sure we will manage it."

Robin looked sharply at Oliver; he could see that he was finding walking quite difficult.

"Are you sure you're alright, Ol? Perhaps we shouldn't have come."

"Are you kidding? Pain or no pain, I wouldn't miss this for the world. I can't have you having adventures without me."

By this time, the lads had just about reached the Hemlock Stone. They couldn't get really close to it, for there was a fence around it. This was to prevent anyone climbing up it as the lower part was sandstone and had crumbled as a result of being climbed on.

It is said that many years ago it was called the 'Himlech Stone'. Folklore said that a giant had thrown it there; other tales said it was called the 'Hemlock Stone' after the Hemlock used by witches that used to meet around the Stone back in medieval times. Whatever the truth about it, it was certainly a curiosity just standing there all on its own in the middle of a hillside. As geologists have found that surrounding areas are comprised of similar rock layers, it can be supposed that it was simply left there by the last Ice Age. However, it really seemed to have an air of mystery about it and the tales lingered.

The boys watched a group of people lingering around the stone, looking at it and reading the information that was on a board. Eventually, the group wandered away and, seeing they were at last alone, the boys joined fingers, recited the clue and Robin put on his ring once more...

Chapter 25

The Final Meeting

It took a few moments for the boys to realise where they were. It was dark as it had been last time they were here. They appeared to be standing in the middle of nothing; they couldn't see anything around them. It was Robin who realised where they were.

"Crumbs, Ol – we're on top of the Hemlock Stone – oh heck, it makes me feel funny."

"Gosh Rob, you're right – wicked!"

At that moment, they heard the murmur of voices below them and, as if by mutual decision, the boys both laid down on their fronts. They peered carefully over the edge. Below them, they saw once again the same cloaked and hooded group of people that they had seen before. They both hoped they wouldn't have to witness another sacrifice. Fortunately it seemed the meeting, or whatever it was, had finished and the group was preparing to leave. The boys were considerably relieved; they really didn't want to tangle with these shady characters! It seemed that this was not what they were here for.

However, there was still the tricky problem of what they were going to do; they were stuck on the top of the Hemlock Stone and they had no idea why they were here. They watched silently as the procession of dark figures walked away, their torches now flaring in a line, getting smaller and smaller until they had disappeared completely. Now what?

Suddenly, they realised they were not alone on the Stone – there were two dark figures standing not far behind them! They scrambled to their feet, hearts thumping. Robin thought wildly of jumping off the huge rock, would he break his whole body or would the ring save him?

"Greetings, Ring Wearer." It was a voice Robin recognised – Edric! With relief, he stepped closer to the man who had spoken. Oliver tapped the staff on the ground and light flared from it as it had in the cave.

"Ah, I see that you have discovered one of the Staff's uses."

"What happens now; why are we here?"

"You are here to give to me the items you were sent to gather, the Staff and the magic Sphere, also the Amulet that I gave to you for safekeeping. You have done very well."

"Why do we give them to you? What will you do with them?"

"They belong to me. They got lost in time; although I knew where they were, I was not able to get them. I sent you to gather for me what is mine."

"How do we know that we can trust you? And don't you need the ring as well?" Oliver had obviously been thinking things through.

"Ah, a young man with determination - you are a fitting wearer for the Amulet, my young friend!"

Oliver stared at him.

"How did you know that I wear the amulet?"

"I know everything!" Edric laughed softly. "Now, my brave young friends, please give me the Items. The amulet first, please." He held his hand out towards Oliver. Robin looked at his ring; he knew it would tell him if things were okay. Sure enough, the ring glowed bright and golden; in fact, it looked more beautiful than it ever had before. It was witness enough.

"Give him the amulet, Ol. the ring says it's safe."

Robin watched as Oliver took the amulet from up his sleeve and handed it to Edric. He put it on his own arm; it fitted perfectly.

"Thank you. Now the golden sphere, if you please, Ring Wearer."

Robin drew the golden ball from his pocket. Like the ring, it glowed brightly; it hardly needed the light that came from the staff. Robin was reluctant to give it up; after all, they had not yet found out what magic it held...

Edric cupped the ball in his left hand, held out in front of him. He then held out his hand for the staff. Oliver stepped forward again and handed it to him.

With the ball in his left hand, the staff in his right hand, Edric lifted up both his arms and chanted:

"Behold Power Instruments three,

Restore full glory unto me."

He tapped the staff on the ground, and they saw a burst of light so bright they could hardly bear to keep their eyes open. Before their startled gaze it was as if a film was being rewound in front of them, for they saw the dragon, the golden ball in the cave, the hermit and then Sir Ralf, then the coven of witches and warlocks and Edric and Orvin running away. They disappeared suddenly and then there was Edric as a glorious figure standing before them. His hair was golden and flowing, his blue eyes were bright and clear and his robes were pure white. The Staff was now bright gold like the ball and Edric stood, holding the two items as a king would hold an orb and sceptre. The previously shadowy Orvin stood by his side, dressed in robes befitting a royal servant.

The boys were so shocked they fell immediately to their knees and bowed low, their hands locked behind their heads.

Chapter 26

Answers

"Arise, Ring Wearer."

Robin looked up and he got on his feet slowly, all the while looking into the eyes of the beautiful Edric standing before him. Oliver stayed where he was, just in case, although he did venture to raise his eyes from the ground.

Robin was speechless, although there were many questions he wanted to ask.

"I perceive you have questions. Ask."

"I, er, that is, who are you? Are you a king?"

"I may be, I may not be. I am The Adventurer. I am Master of The Ring but also the servant."

Robin was somewhat puzzled by this.

"I am the creator of the Ring. Now I serve it. But there is no one greater than I."

"How do you serve the ring?"

"I am The Adventurer. I provide the adventures the ring chooses to give."

"Does that mean the adventures we've had were not real? That it was you all the time?"

"You and your friend worked out how to get the staff didn't you? And you rescued him from the dragon. Oh yes, my friend, your adventures were real. I have much to thank you for. I would not have been restored without you."

"How is that? If you are so powerful, how could you have needed our help?"

"Well, when you first met me, I was running from the coven, yes?"

"Yes, but you are much more powerful than they; why did you need to run?"

"Because they knew I had stolen the amulet!"

"You stole the amulet? But it belongs to you, doesn't it?"

"Oh yes, it belongs to me. But Bowen the Black is a greedy and powerful man; he and his followers somehow managed to break through into my world. He had found out in some way about the staff, the sphere, and the amulet. He knew there is great power, much more than he would ever have, in the three things.

"When I found him in my palace, I used my magic to fling the sphere, the ring and the staff far away in time so they couldn't get them; unfortunately, they were upon me before I could do the same with the amulet. I barely escaped with my life with my faithful servant Orvin and they got away with the amulet. Without the power of the four items, I became stuck as you saw me, my own time.

"I knew where the other two items were, I was just unable to get them back without the Ring. I knew the Ring would find a valiant person who would be able to restore them to me.

"In the meantime, Orvin and I had managed to steal the Amulet back and were fleeing for our lives when we came upon you. If I had had the chance I would have thrown the Amulet too and the Ring would have sent you to find it. However, since you came upon us while it was still in my possession and knowing you would return to your own time, I gave you the Amulet so that you could keep it safe where they couldn't get it until the other Items were restored and brought together."

Oliver was so intrigued by Edric's story that he quite forgot he was kneeling in fear. This time he wanted to know something.

"Why didn't you ask for the Ring back?"

Edric turned towards him as if he had forgotten Oliver was there.

"Ah, the Ring Wearer's companion speaks! The Items of Power have names. They are called: 'The Staff of Faith', the 'The Amulet of Determination' and 'The Sphere of Courage'. They are so named because in order to adventure properly, you need those things: Determination, Courage and Faith. In order to secure the Items of Power you used all those things, for without them you would not have succeeded. The Ring, however, is a bit different. It is certainly called The Ring of Power, but the Ring chooses the wearer, not the other way round. It will go to whoever is the right person. It will stay and serve that person, providing for him what he (or she) needs at the time. It will stay for as long as it feels necessary. One day it will simply be gone; or you will still have a ring but the power within it will no longer be there. It will leave when you have found your own power."

Edric was looking at Robin as he said this. Robin was struggling to understand.

"Does that mean it could take us on other adventures?"

"It may well, depending on what is needed. But it will also stay with you as you live your life, for life itself is a great adventure. You have to have the right attitude to life, to overcome obstacles and difficulties. With determination, courage and faith you can achieve anything you want."

Robin nodded, thinking hard.

"What are we supposed to have faith in?"

"That is for you to decide for yourself."

Edric stepped towards Oliver and pointed the staff at his sprained ankle.

"Since you were injured in my service, I will heal your ankle." A blue flame seemed to shoot from the staff, spreading around Oliver's foot, making it look like it was engulfed in fire. It went as suddenly as it came and Oliver moved his foot around experimentally.

"It doesn't hurt anymore. Thank you very much."

Edric bowed his head a moment, graciously.

"Won't you heal Robin's leg too?" Oliver asked.

"I cannot do that I'm afraid because Robin's leg is one of his obstacles to overcome. However, he will find that it will become as nothing in time. In the meantime, the Ring will help him."

Robin nodded again; he understood. He had one more question.

"How is it that sometimes the Ring just helps me with strength and other times it has moved us in time?"

"I think I know the answer to that Rob." Oliver broke in. "It's because it has more than one power; it does what you need at the time."

"Very good young master; you have understood."

"I understand that it helps us to understand language too, which is why you are using our modern speech instead of that of your time," said Robin.

"That is correct also, Ring Wearer."

The boys stood looking at Edric, still unable to believe all that had happened; they had much to think about.

"And now I think you must go home, for I perceive that the Ring Wearer's parents are on their way back for you."

He waved his staff, and, before they had a chance to blink, the two boys were standing in the car park, waiting, just as Carole and Roy drew up in the car.

"Hello you two, that was good timing! Did you have a good time?"

"Yes, it was really great; thank you so much for letting us come."

As the boys climbed into the car, they suddenly realised that, yet again, they had not even touched their food.

Chapter 27

A Satisfying Payback

When they got home, the boys sneaked their bags upstairs; they wanted to eat their food without having to explain why they still had it.

They went into Robin's room, shut the door and proceeded to unpack the food and eat. They sat on the floor so as not to get any crumbs in the beds. They discussed the happenings of the morning; they were still incredulous and what they had seen and what Edric had told them. As they cleared up after eating and Robin turned to his computer, he said:

"Wow - look Ol!"

Oliver came to see what Robin was pointing at. There, on the computer table were three tiny gold objects — an amulet, a ball and a staff. As they picked them up, they heard Edric's voice, very quietly:

"Determination, Courage and Faith - always keep them, always remember them and always do them. If you ever need help, they will be there for you."

The boys looked around as if they expected to see Edric, but they saw nothing.

"That's amazing – do you think they are the actual ones?"

"Well, I have no idea. But I do know I will need to keep them very safe," said Robin.

"That's for sure. And if the ring takes us on other adventures we must remember to take them with us," replied Oliver.

"You betcha!"

Robin and Oliver held the objects and looked at them closely, turning them around in their hands. Eventually, Robin took all three and popped them in the leather pouch that he still had and then in his box of treasures that he kept on a shelf and turned the key.

Oliver went home the next day; the adults were amazed that his ankle was completely better so suddenly.

"That's boys for you," they laughed. The boys looked at each other and grinned.

*****

Back at school, Robin had a most trying week. Mr Brown was even more determined to make him suffer. He really seemed to have taken against Robin and it didn't matter how hard the boy tried, it was never good enough. When writing about 'What I Did in the Holidays' Robin wrote about his and Oliver's adventures, leaving out some important bits, like about Edric.

Mr Brown was very scathing about it, saying it was a good story but obviously he'd had such a boring holiday that he had to make stuff up. Robin knew that his proper teacher, Mr James, would have praised him for his imaginative story; after all, he couldn't really expect anyone to believe what he'd written.

He gazed at Mr Brown's braces – why did he wear braces in this day and age? It was something that old men wore. Mr Brown was not all that old – and his braces were bright red, blue and gold striped – they were awful! It seemed he had a 'thing' about braces for he had several sets of them that he'd worn at different times.

If lessons were bad, PE was a nightmare. Friday afternoons were always PE on the field. Before they went out there, Mr Brown told the class that this was his last session with them, for Mr James was well again and was returning to work next week. He was not pleased at the cheer that went up on that announcement and he put the class through an awful time on the field. He had several children in tears and even those who usually liked and enjoyed PE were completely exhausted. He knew that the headmaster wasn't in that day; he felt he could do what he wanted.

As for Robin, well, however much determination and courage he applied it was never good enough for Mr Brown, who roared at him all the time. Robin refused to cry, although he felt like it. One of the bigger boys, who was good at sport, tried hard to tell Mr Brown to lay off Robin; in fact, he completely lost his temper and shouted at the teacher and as a result got sent into the school in disgrace. Robin was struggling for breath; he hardly knew what he was doing. He was on the verge of collapse when the deputy head came onto the field and took Robin away. The boy who had been sent in had gone straight to him and told him what was happening. Robin was so thankful as he struggled for breath in the sick bay.

Robin joined his class when they came back. Later, when everyone had left to go home, Mr Brown was marking the last of the work before he left. Robin was gathering his things in the cloakroom; because he was still not feeling too good he had let the other children go first before he attempted to go in for his things. He pulled on his coat. As he did so, Mr Brown came into the cloakroom. He looked at Robin.

"What are you still doing here boy? Are you so fond of being here? Do you want some more exercise eh? Toughen you up."

Robin stared at the man's chest; hating him. This was a new feeling for Robin, he didn't hate anyone. As he gazed at the garish braces in front of him, he heard a noise coming from his coat pocket – the ring! That's funny, he was sure he'd left it at home... he slipped his finger into it.

"Do you know, SIR, that you are a bully? Bullies should not be teachers. You are not fit to be a teacher. Mr James gets us to do a lot without being like you are. You obviously know nothing about asthmatics either. What is the matter with you and what did I ever do to you that you have picked on me the way you have?"

Robin watched with interest and curious detachment as the man's face changed from white to red to purple.

"Why you rude little boy - how dare you speak to me like that?"

"I dare because you need telling."

Suddenly, as Robin looked at the braces, he remembered something his granddad told him about something he did once. He looked behind the man at the coat pegs. They were old fashioned, iron and curly, very strong, for this was a Victorian building. Some of the pegs were too high up for the present-day children. Dare he do it? Would the ring let him?

Before Mr Brown knew what was happening, Robin had lifted him clean off his feet and hooked his braces on a couple of coat pegs. He looked ridiculous hanging there, his feet half a metre off the ground, his face again turning all shades of red and purple as he spluttered with anger and incredulousness.

"Looks like those PE lessons paid off after all, don't you think sir?"

Robin ran out of the school, leaping in the air and punching it in laughter. He knew the man wouldn't be there long because the caretaker would find him; but he may have to have those stupid braces cut to get him down!

Just think how silly they will think him if he says Robin put him there – he will find out how it feels to not be believed. He was a bully and he needed to find out how it felt – well, he would now wouldn't he?

Robin knew he had been naughty really, but somehow he just couldn't help himself. And, as he ran out of the playground, he was sure he could hear Edric The Adventurer laughing.

Look out for the next adventure with Robin and Oliver!

21620551R00088

Printed in Great Britain
by Amazon